Raven's Call

and More Northwest Coast Stories

Written and Illustrated

by

Robert James Challenger

Heritage House Publishing Company Ltd.
#108 – 17665 66A Avenue
Surrey, BC V3S 2A7
www.heritagehouse.ca

Library and Archives Canada Cataloguing in Publication
Challenger, Robert James, 1953–
Raven's call and more Northwest Coast stories

ISBN 978-1-895811-91-9

1. Nature stories, Canadian (English)* 2. Children's stories, Canadian (English)* I. Title.

PS8555.H277R38 1999 jC813'.54 C99-910740-2
PZ7.C3498Ra 1999

All illustrations: Robert James Challenger
Book design and layout: Darlene Nickull
Editor: Rhonda Bailey

Printed in Canada

This book has been printed with FSC-certified, acid-free papers, processed chlorine free and printed with vegetable based inks.

Heritage House acknowledges the financial support for its publishing program from the Government of Canada through the Book Publishing Industry Development Program (BPIDP), Canada Council for the Arts, and the British Columbia Arts Council.

Canada Council for the Arts
Conseil des Arts du Canada

Dedicated to my dad,
Robert Adams (Bob) Challenger
1924 – 1998

A man who knew his calling
was to love his family.

Other books by Robert James Challenger

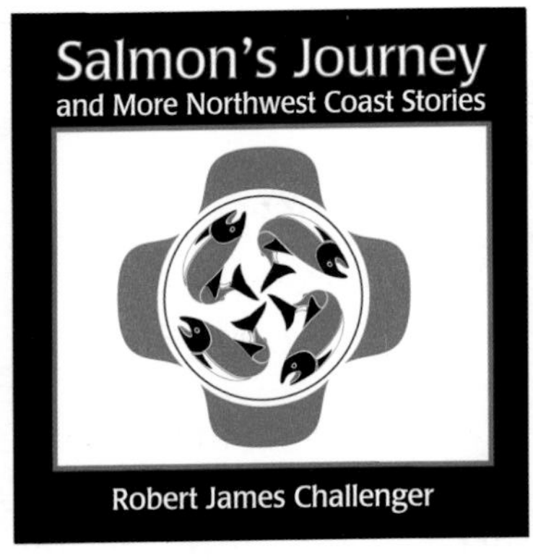

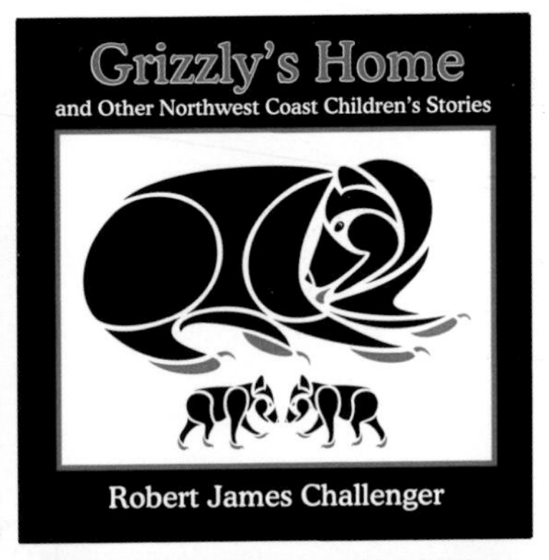

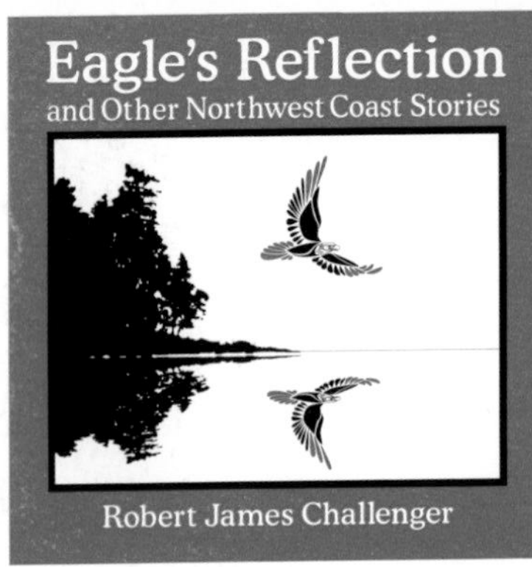

Nature's Circle
and Other Northwest Coast Children's Stories
ISBN 978-1-894384-77-3

Salmon's Journey
and More Northwest Coast Stories
ISBN 978-1-894384-34-6

Grizzly's Home
and Other Northwest Coast Children's Stories
ISBN 978-1-894384-94-0

Eagle's Reflection
and Other Northwest Coast Stories
ISBN 978-1-895811-07-0

Orca's Family
and More Northwest Coast Stories
ISBN 978-1-895811-39-1

All $9.95

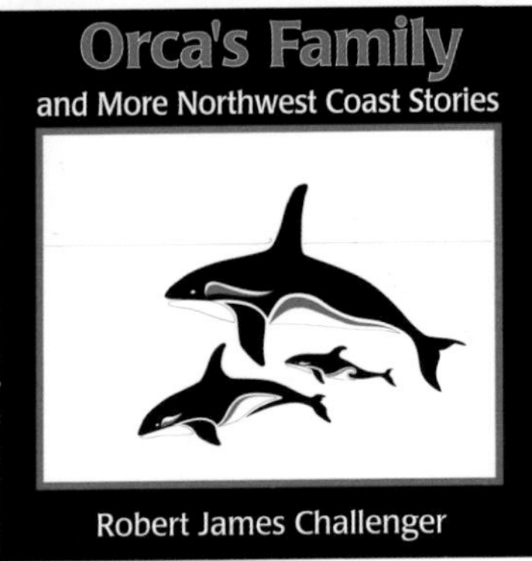

Wonderful Northwest Coast stories for kids … Jim Challenger is a real artist as his book demonstrates.

—Ron MacIssac, Shaw Cable's "What's Happening?"

I really loved your stories that you read to us. I really got the feeling of what you meant in your magical writing. Thank you for coming to our school to make us feel joyful. I enjoyed your stories!! Sincerely,

—Josey L. (Age 8)

Modern day fables are the right length … knows how to write for the oral storyteller; the written words slip easily off the tongue.

—*Times Colonist*

Challenger's prose bears a deliberate resemblance to First Nations oral traditions: humans and nature interact freely, and both are capable of folly, repentance, and wisdom. In his artwork, Challenger also embraces West Coast Aboriginal culture by portraying his characters in exquisite Haida-style prints. Highly recommended.

—Steve Pitt, *Canadian Book Review Annual*

Contents

Raven's Call

The sun was rising in the east and an early morning mist was rising from the ocean as Father and Mother paddled their boat around a point. Both of them were deep in thought as the boat silently slipped through the still water. No words were spoken.

Off in the distance a small, rocky island with ragged, windswept trees came into view. At the top of one tree was a nest, and as the boat went by the island they could see Raven sitting in the nest watching them.

Raven called to them, "Where are you going?"

Father pointed and said, "We are heading to the gap between that island and the island that your nest is on. We are going to fish for salmon."

Raven flew down and landed on the boat.

Raven said, "That is not what I meant when I asked you where you are going, I meant where are you going in your life?"

Father thought for a few minutes, then replied, "I don't really know. We are always trying to find food for our family and to teach our children the lessons we have learned."

Mother added, "We spend all our time just taking care of each other."

Raven said, "It sounds to me like you do know where you are going.

"Your destiny will be the result of the decisions you make throughout your lives.

"You have decided that your family is important to you. I know that whatever happens, you will be satisfied with where you end up because you have learned to make decisions based on what is truly important in all our lives, which is caring about others."

Raven smiled at them, spread his wings, and flew back to take care of the young ones in the nest.

Mother said to Father, "Raven is right. We do know where we want to go, and it is a good feeling to know we are headed in the right direction."

Mountain Goat's Path

Grandmother and her daughter sat watching the grandchildren playing out behind the camp.

The children were building a fort in Maple Tree. They helped each other lift up pieces of wood for the floor. They all laughed when the blanket they were using for their roof blew away and landed in a puddle. When the smaller ones could not climb up, the bigger children got down and helped them. They all shared the lunch between them.

Grandmother smiled and said to her daughter, "Watching them reminds me of the story of Mountain Goat.

"Mountain Goat lives high up in the steep, rocky mountains. It is both a safe and dangerous place to raise a family. It is safe because the pathways are so narrow and steep that hunters cannot easily find them. But the same pathways are also dangerous for Mountain Goat's children because they could easily fall.

"Every day, Mountain Goat tells her young ones to carefully choose their pathway and place each hoof onto solid ground. When they are out walking, she tells them to follow her so they will know the safest route and learn to put their feet exactly where she does. As Mountain Goat walks, she carefully chooses her route and each spot to step on because she knows that the little ones following behind are watching and relying on her to keep them safe.

"By the time they are grown up, the children have followed her example so many times that they are ready to go out on their own and eventually to teach their own children."

Grandmother looked at her daughter and said, "Your children are already starting to follow the good examples you are setting. They are helping each other, enjoying laughter, taking care of each other, and sharing. They learn both from what you tell them to do and from what they see you doing every day. And, just like Mountain Goat, they always see you carefully walk along the same path that you talk about."

Mouse's Worries

Father and Grandfather were out fishing on the bay. As Father rowed the boat, he said to Grandfather, "I am really concerned about the weather.

"What if we do not get enough rain for my garden to grow? What if a storm comes and too much rain falls and floods my field? What if it gets so cold that my plants freeze and die before harvest time? What if it gets too hot and my plants all shrivel up? What would we eat?"

Grandfather asked, "Have I ever told you the story of Mouse?"

"No, I don't think so," said Father.

"Well," said Grandfather, "Mouse lives deep in the forest near the big meadow. He has lived there for many years, and he has built a home and raised many children.

"Mouse used to worry about the weather, just like you do. He worried that the rain would fall too fast and flood his home. He worried that it would be too dry for the new meadow grass to grow each spring. He worried about forest fires when it was hot and he worried about too much snow when it was cold.

"One day, he was telling Raven about all his worries, and Raven asked him, 'What would you do if they all came true?'

"Mouse replied, 'Well, if it really did start raining too hard I would have to move to a burrow on higher ground. If it did get too dry for the meadow grass to come up then I would probably just go down by the river and get grass from there. If a forest fire started, I could dig deeper down into my burrow, where I would be safe. And if too much snow fell, it really wouldn't matter as long as I had enough food stored away for the winter.'

"Then Raven asked Mouse, 'What can you do to stop the weather from happening?'

"Mouse thought for a minute, then replied, 'There is nothing I can do. If things happen they happen. These are natural events and nobody can control them.'

"Raven smiled and said, 'So, let me see what we have here. You are worrying about a lot of things you admit you can do nothing about. And even if these things happen, you would always find a way to survive.'

"Mouse looked embarrassed. He said, 'You are right, Raven. I have been wasting time and energy worrying about things I cannot control. Starting now, I will use that time and energy to build a new burrow on higher ground, look for other places where grass grows, dig my burrow a little deeper, and put away some extra food each winter.'"

Father said, "That is a good lesson. No matter how much I worry about the weather, what happens will happen. I'll just have to be prepared, accept what comes, and make the best of it."

Chipmunk's Favour

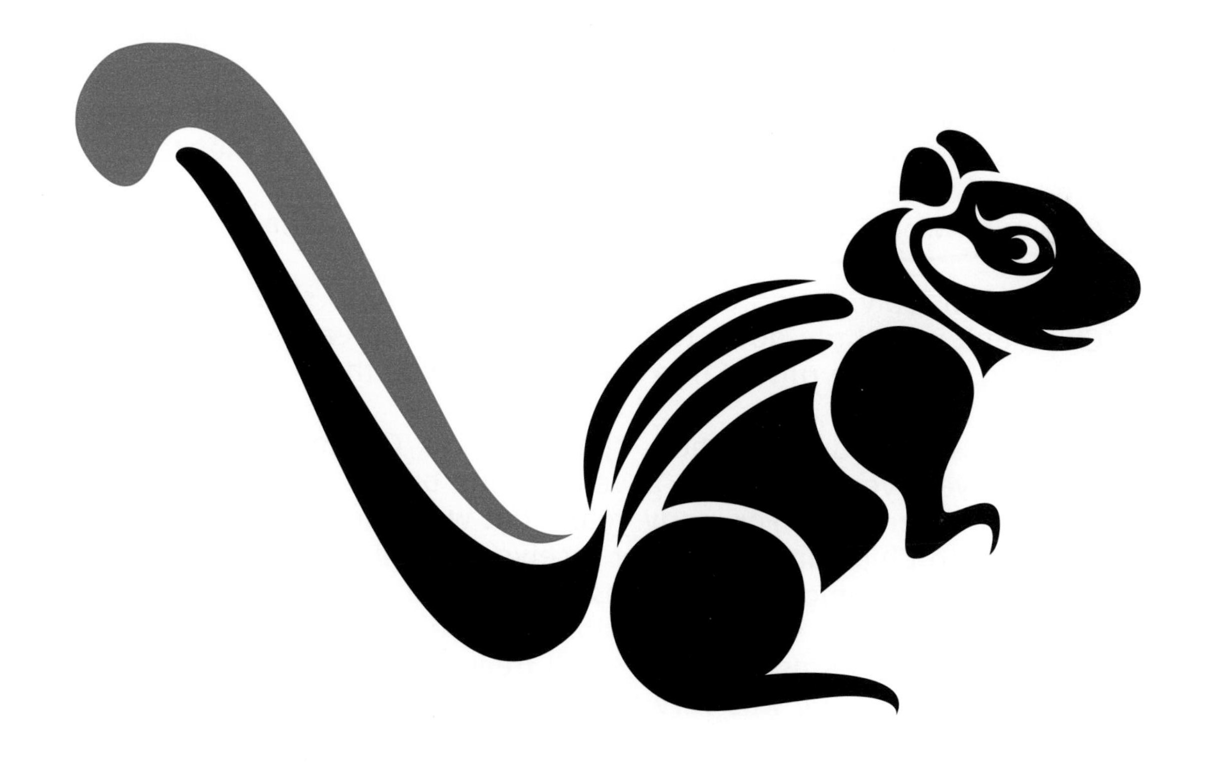

Grandmother sat on the beach listening to Grandson and Granddaughter. The two children were arguing about who would go up to the house to get some water to drink.

Grandson said, "I went up to get the blanket to sit on, so you have to go this time."

Granddaughter replied, "But, last time I went to get the water. It is your turn."

Grandmother called them over and said, "Sit with me for a while. I have a story to tell you.

"For many years, Chipmunk scrambled up Tree's trunk and out along his branches to where his ripe cones grow. Chipmunk nibbled the stems, and one by one the cones would fall to the ground below.

"Chipmunk would always remember to stop and say, 'Thank you, Tree.'

"Tree would reply, 'You are welcome. I have plenty to share with you.'

"Chipmunk would run down to the ground, pick up each cone, take the seeds out, and then run off into the forest to hide them in his underground burrows."

Grandson said to Grandmother, "That's not fair. Chipmunk got all Tree's seeds every year and never gave anything back."

Grandmother replied, "For many years that was true. Tree continued to give his seeds to Chipmunk and never received anything in return.

"One hot, dry summer, a storm crossed over the forest and a bolt of lightning hit the ground, starting a terrible wildfire. The fire burned for many days, and afterwards all of the small trees in the forest were gone.

"Tree survived, but he was very sad that the forest no longer had any young trees.

"Chipmunk came to the rescue. He went to all his burrows and took out the seeds he had stored. He ran about the forest and planted them in the warm ashes. For days he continued to plant the seeds he had been given over the years by Tree.

"When the rains finally came, the seeds sprouted, and by the next spring there were thousands of new trees growing in the forest. Tree was very happy.

"He said to Chipmunk, 'I am glad that I shared all my seeds with you. Thank you for starting a new forest for all of us to enjoy.'"

Grandmother turned to the children. "You see, you cannot count how many favours one person does against how many the other has done. Chipmunk paid Tree back with one big favour that repaid the many small ones Tree had given him.

"Perhaps you two need to think the same way. Instead of competing against each other you could both look for ways to try to help each other. Trust that in the long run you will be repaid for your kindness."

Hawk's Eyes and Ears

Granddaughter walked hand-in-hand with Grandfather along the beach. Great ocean waves swept up and down the sand.

Above them, Hawk soared in the blue sky. Bright sunlight shone off his eyes like two sparkling diamonds. He cocked his head to one side then the other, listening to the sounds below. Once, he let out a short screech to let his mate know where he was.

Grandfather said to Granddaughter, "Hawk is having a good time looking and listening from up there. Tell me, Granddaughter, what do you see and hear today?"

They stopped walking, and after a moment Granddaughter said, "I see the waves turning into white foam as they rush up the smooth beach, which reminds me that each day only lasts a moment and then is gone. I see the wind blowing the branches and making them dance high up in the green trees, which makes me want to dance, too. And I see two sets of footprints in the sand behind us from you and me walking down the beach together, which reminds me how much I like being with you."

Grandfather asked, "And what do your hear?"

She replied, "I hear the stones rolling against each other as each wave crashes onto the beach, which tells me the waves are very big today and I should not try to go swimming. I hear Hawk's call to his mate, which reminds me that I need to get home soon. And I hear the wind blowing through the trees, which means the weather might change before long."

She smiled at Grandfather, "And I hear myself talking to you!"

They both laughed and started walking back down the beach towards home.

Grandfather said to her, "You and Hawk are both very wise. You know that with two eyes you can see everything happening in the world if you just take the time to look. And with two ears, you can hear everything if you take the time to listen. The trick is that we all have to remember to stop talking long enough to let our eyes and ears have their turn."

Mother Grouse's Courage

Returning from the meadow, Grandmother and Granddaughter walked along the forest path. It was an early spring morning. The bright sunlight shone down through the high tree branches and made the dewdrops glisten like jewels.

It was quiet in the forest, so the sudden rush of a bird darting out of the trees caused them to jump. Grandmother and Granddaughter stood watching as Mother Grouse limped down the pathway. They started to follow her.

Granddaughter asked, "Is she hurt, Grandmother?"

Grandmother answered, "No, I don't believe she is. I think she has something else in mind."

"Why isn't she afraid of us, like other birds are? Why doesn't she fly away?" Granddaughter asked.

"Look over there, under the bushes, and you will see a nest with her chicks in it," said Grandmother. "I think Mother Grouse is leading us away from her nest in order to protect her babies. She is pretending to be hurt in the hope that we will go after her and leave her young ones alone."

When they were well past the nest site, Mother Grouse jumped up and flew back through the trees to her nest.

Granddaughter called to Mother Grouse, "You are a very brave bird. When I have children I will try to be as fearless as you are."

Grandmother smiled at her, "I'm sure you will. It's not that hard to be courageous when you are protecting the ones you love most."

Dolphin's Lies

Grandmother sat listening to the young children playing. She noticed that Grandson seemed to be telling some awfully big tales about things he had done.

She heard him say, "I caught a fish so big that Grandfather could not lift it into our boat."

Then he said, "I climbed a big mountain all by myself and slept on the top of it overnight."

When he started to say "I fought Grizzly Bear..."Grandmother had heard enough.

She called him over and said to him, "I think you need to hear the story about Dolphin's Lies.

"Many years ago, there were dolphins who swam in our bay, jumping and splashing in the waves.

"Once, when Eagle was flying overhead, Dolphin said, 'I am so fast that I once jumped over the sun.'

"Eagle did not reply.

"Dolphin said to him, 'One day I dove so deep that I came up on the other side of the world.'

"Eagle still did not reply.

"Then Dolphin bragged to Eagle, 'When I am hungry I wait until Grandfather has a fish on his line, and then I steal it. When he asks me if I took his fish I say it was one of the others.'

"Eagle finally replied to Dolphin, 'Each time you tell a lie the weight of your dishonesty builds up inside you. Soon you won't be a sleek Dolphin. Instead you will transform into a big, slow Humpback Whale. The weight of all your lies will drag you to the bottom of the ocean, where you will have to spend the rest of your days alone in the darkness.'

"Dolphin said to Eagle, 'I don't want that to happen. What can I do?'

"Eagle said, 'From now on, you must always be honest. If you do, then you will be able to stay as a Dolphin.'

Grandmother looked at Grandson and said, "Don't let the weight of many lies drag you down. Be honest with other people and show them that you can be trusted – then they can like you for who you really are, instead of who you pretend to be."

How Bear Became Black

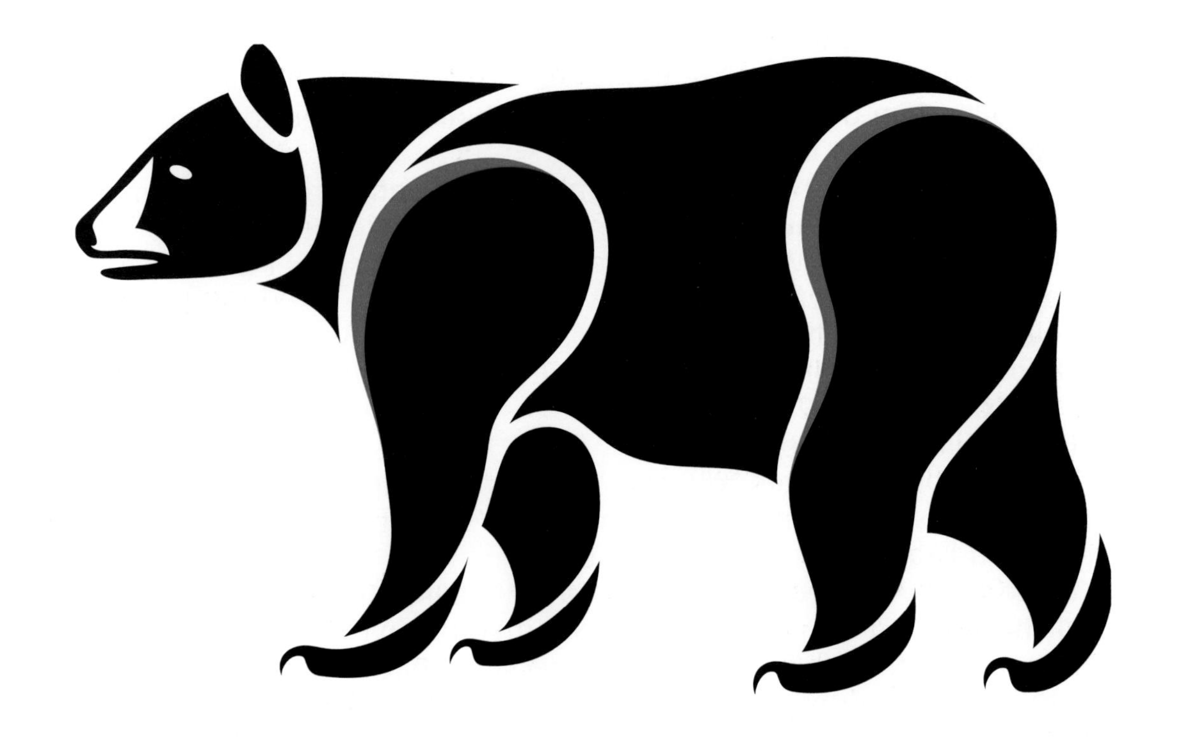

Grandson sat on a rock looking over the bay. He was feeling very sad, and tears ran down his face. When Grandfather came by, he could clearly see that the young boy was troubled.

Grandfather quietly said, "It is a warm sunny day, bright with light sparkling off the waves in the ocean. What could be making you feel so sad?"

Grandson replied, "My brother gets all the attention. Everyone always notices him because he is so tall."

Grandfather sat down beside the boy and began to tell the story of Black Bear.

"Many years ago, all bears were white. That was a good thing for bears who lived where it was always snowing. They blended in and were hard to notice. It made it easy for them to hunt food and to avoid being hunted themselves.

"But for bears who lived in the forest, it was not a good thing. Their white fur made them too easy to see. Animals could see Forest Bear from far away and would always have time to run for shelter. When hunters were out looking for Forest Bear, they could easily find him because his fur stood out against the dark trees.

"Raven felt sorry for Forest Bear, so he transformed his white fur to the deepest black of the night sky. Now, as Black Bear, he can live happily among the trees.

"In return for Raven's favour, Black Bear made it a point always to help other animals. Over the years, Black Bear has become an honoured creature of the forest because of all the things he does for others.

"You see," said Grandfather to Grandson, "It is often easier to get along if the way you look does not make you stand out too much from others. Then, just like Black Bear, you can stand out because of the good things you do rather than because of how you look."

Blue Jay's Colours

Granddaughter was feeding some small birds by throwing them seeds she had collected. Suddenly a large black bird flashed down out of the trees. It cawed loudly and scared all the other birds.

Crow began gobbling all the food, and whenever the other birds tried to get some, he would chase them away.

Granddaughter said to Crow, "Well, you are being greedy, aren't you?"

Crow said to her, "I can take anything I want because I am bigger."

Granddaughter said, "My friend Eagle is going to have to teach you a lesson."

She called out, "Eagle! Please come and teach Crow to share."

Eagle heard her. With a screech, he dove out of the sky and began to chase Crow. Higher and higher he chased him until Crow was so high up in the sky that he ran into the clouds. The clouds began to stick to Crow, turning some of his feathers white.

Eagle asked him, "Are you ready to share?"

Crow called back, "No."

So Eagle continued to chase him until Crow reached the blue layer that gives the sky its colour. As he passed through it, some of the colour rubbed off onto him. Now Crow's feathers were part black, part white, and part blue.

Eagle asked, "Are you ready to share yet?"

Crow answered, "No, I am still not going to share."

Eagle chased Crow until he got so close to the sun that Crow started to shrink from the heat. Crow got smaller and smaller until he was only half his original size.

Crow finally called out to Eagle, "Please, stop chasing me. My feathers are black, white, and blue and I am too small to scare any other birds. I will share with them now."

Eagle said to him, "Good. I am glad you have changed your mind along with your colour and size. From now on, we will all call you Blue Jay."

They both flew back down to the ground where Blue Jay shared Granddaughter's seeds with all the other little birds

Granddaughter said to Eagle, "Thank you for helping. Now, whenever others see Blue Jay's colours, they will remember that it is important to share with others."

Squirrel's Point of View

Grandfather and two of his grandchildren sat by the campfire. The two children were arguing with each other. As time went by their voices became louder and angrier.

Grandfather listened as the first child said, "The forest is protected by Eagle. He is bigger than Raven. He can fly higher and faster."

The other child replied, "No, you are wrong. Raven is the protector of the forest. He doesn't need to be fast because the trees are not moving around. And he doesn't need to fly way up in the air because the forest is down here on the ground."

Finally Grandfather said, "Maybe you both are right."

The children looked at him with puzzled looks. One said, "How can both of us be right at the same time?"

Grandfather replied with a story.

"Many years ago, I heard Grey Squirrel and Red Squirrel describe a place they had visited.

"Grey Squirrel said, 'I climbed up a tall tree and from there I could see the valley below. There was dense forest all around a beautiful green lake.'

"Red Squirrel said, 'No, that's not what it was like at all. I climbed up the very same tree and was sitting right behind you. I saw a tall mountain with alpine meadows full of flowers.'

"Grey Squirrel said, 'I could see Moose feeding in the valley meadow.'

"Red Squirrel replied, 'I only saw Eagle and Raven soaring in the wind. Are you sure we are talking about the same place?'

"I said to them, 'Perhaps you are, but you don't know it. Grey Squirrel, you said you climbed the same tree and were sitting right behind Red Squirrel. Were you on the other side of the tree?'

"Grey Squirrel thought for a moment then replied, 'Yes, I was.'

"I said to them, 'It seems that all along you were talking about the same place. You were simply describing it from two different points of view because you were on opposite sides of the tree.'"

Grandfather looked at his two grandchildren and said, "You see, perhaps both of you are right too. Eagle and Raven both protect the forest because they work together as a team, listen to each other, and respect each other's point of view."

How Blue Whale Became Big

Grandfather added another piece of wood to the campfire. Sparks danced up into the deep-blue evening sky. The children moved closer to the fire to feel its warmth. The smallest of the children climbed up onto Grandfather's lap and wrapped the old man's coat around himself. The others settled into their places as Grandfather began to tell a story.

"Many years ago, when I was a child, I was not very honest. Sometimes I lied to avoid having to take blame for mistakes I had made. Other times I would take things that were not mine so I did not have to earn them. I was not always reliable, and people learned not to trust me."

One of the small children asked, "But you aren't like that now, Grandfather. When did you change?"

Grandfather replied, "It happened one day when I was out fishing and Blue Whale came up beside my small boat.

"Blue Whale said to me, 'Don't worry. I will not harm you. I have come to talk to you about the value of being honest and trustworthy.'

"'Every time you tell a lie or let others down who trust you, you become smaller in their eyes. If you continue, you will soon become so small that nobody will trust you. You will be so small that it will be as if they can't even see you.'

"I asked Blue Whale, who was so big that my boat and I could fit inside him, 'How can I change?'

"Blue Whale told me, 'Whenever you have to make a decision, look into your heart and make your choice based on what you know is the right thing to do. Once others see that you always try to do the right thing, you will start to grow in their eyes. If you never let them down, then someday, in their eyes, you could grow to be as big as I am.'

"I told Blue Whale, 'You are very big, so I trust and believe what you have told me. From this day on, I will always try to do the right thing so that I can grow big like you.'"

The child sitting in Grandfather's lap pulled the sides of Grandfather's coat closed around him.

His tiny voice came from inside the coat, "Grandfather, you must have told the truth to Blue Whale, because now you are so big I can fit inside you!"

Memories Don't Die

Granddaughter cried as she walked with Grandmother from the forest. They were returning from the place where they had laid to rest the little girl's dog that had died. It was a very sad time.

As they entered the house, the little girl sobbed, "Grandmother, I miss my dog. Now I will never see her again. She is gone forever."

Grandmother lit the candle on the table, and its soft glow spread across the room.

She sat down at the table with the child and said to her, "It is true. You will never see your pet again. But she is not gone. She is still here with us, just like she was last week."

The girl stopped crying and asked, "What do you mean? I can't see her, so she can't be here."

Grandmother took Granddaughter's hand and then she leaned over and blew out the candle, leaving them in darkness.

She said, "Now, you cannot see me. Does that mean I am not here with you?"

The girl answered, "Well, I cannot see you but I can feel your hand holding mine, so I know you are still here."

Grandmother lit the candle again. She stood up and walked into the next room. Then she asked, "If I am in the kitchen, where you cannot reach out and touch me, does it mean I am not here?"

The little one answered, "I know you are here in the house because I can still hear you."

Grandmother came back into the room and asked, "How about last summer when I was away on my trip to the other island where you could not touch, hear, or see me? Did it mean I was not still here in the same world with you?"

The girl replied, "I knew you were here because when I thought about you I could remember what you looked like, hear what your voice sounded like, and even remember what it felt like to hold your hand."

Grandmother asked her, "Don't you have memories about your pet? When you think of her, can't you see her still – running in the grass, or barking in excitement whenever you came home? Can't you remember how it felt to run your fingers through her soft fur?"

Granddaughter smiled a little and answered, "Yes, I can. You are right. It is like when she was in the other room or out roaming by herself in the field."

Grandmother smiled and said, "You see, the real difference after a death is that you will not have any new memories to add to the ones you already have. And that is sad. But the lost one can always be here with you as long as you hold onto your memories of past times spent together."

Caribou's Journey

Grandfather stood up and slung a pack on his back. He and Grandson had a long way to go to reach their campsite, and the daylight hours lasted only so long.

Grandson complained, "Grandfather, it is such a long way to the camp – it seems like we will never get there. I think we should just stop and make camp here."

Grandfather replied, "Put on your pack, and as we walk I'll tell you the story of Caribou."

"Every year the Caribou face the challenge of a long migration from their winter home in the south to their summer home in the far north. The journey takes many weeks. They walk across flat plains and through narrow valleys. They climb high mountain passes and swim across wide lakes. Along the way, many of the baby Caribou are born and must quickly learn to walk or be left behind.

"For the adult Caribou it is easier because they know they have successfully completed the journey before. But for the little Caribou it is a new experience.

"When the little ones complain about being tired, Mother Caribou asks them, 'Can't you take one more step?'

"The little ones say, 'Well, yes, I can take a step.'

"'Well,' she tells them, 'A long journey is only one small step followed by another. Put all your small steps together and soon you will be there.'"

Grandfather put his hand on Grandson's shoulder and said, "You see, any long journey in life is possible. The trick is not to think of the whole thing at once. Instead, break it down and take the first step. Then take the one that follows. If you do, you will be surprised at how far you can go."

Crab's Way

Grandfather and Grandson were chopping firewood for the winter ahead. They worked hard, and sweat dripped from them as they piled the wood in the shed near the house.

While they worked, Grandson asked Grandfather for some advice.

He said, "Last week I had an argument with my friend. Now I don't know what to do. He is a good person and I do not want to lose his friendship. Should I give in to him, even though I believe I am right, or should I stand my ground, even though it means I will lose a good friend?"

Grandfather replied, "Perhaps the story of Crab will help you decide what to do.

"One day, Crab was walking along the beach and saw some food over on the other side of the channel. Crab's problem was that the tide was coming in, so the current in the channel was very fast.

"First, Crab tried to walk against the current. He made a little headway, but it was very difficult. Soon he was too tired to keep going.

"Then he tried walking with the current. It was much faster and easier, but he soon realized he wasn't getting any closer to the other side of the channel.

"Finally, he tried walking sideways to the current. It was not as easy as going with the current, but also not as hard as going against it. Slowly he worked his way across the channel and came out where he wanted to be."

Grandfather put his hand on Grandson's shoulder and said to him, "You and your friend have a similar channel to cross.

"You could continue fighting against each other, but all that does is waste a lot of your energy, and your problem will never be solved.

"Or, you could give in and go with the your friend's point of view. Although that may seem like the easiest and fastest solution, it does not solve the problem either. Ultimately you won't end up where you want to be in your friendship.

"Try to work the problem out between you. Then, just like Crab, you will both end up where you want to be."

Sand Dollar's Reminder

The storm from the day before had moved on. The waves were smaller now, and the rain had stopped. Grandfather and Grandson decided to go for a walk on the beach.

They had walked for only a short distance when Grandson bent down and from the wet sand picked up a shell. He washed it off in a shallow pool, revealing a round disk with a flower pattern on the top.

He ran over to Grandfather and asked him, "What is this?"

Grandfather replied, "It is Sand Dollar."

Then he said to the boy, "Let me tell you a story about why you find Sand Dollar here.

"Many years ago, even before I was born, there was a village right where we are standing. In it lived Selfish Man, who was very rich. He had more money than anyone else in the village did. He hardly ever spent any, and he never gave any away.

"Selfish Man stacked his coins up in great piles until his whole tent was full of them.

"One day, Eagle flew down and landed beside Selfish Man.

"Eagle said to him, 'I have just flown in from far out at sea. There is a big storm coming. You need to take some of your money and help build a great stone wall to protect the village from the storm's waves.'

"Selfish Man replied, 'I am not going to spend my money to help everyone else. If the waves wash them away, that is their problem. I will build a wall around my own tent. As long as I am safe, nothing else matters to me.'

"So, that is just what he did. He built a high wooden wall surrounding his tent full of coins.

"Eagle warned the other people, and they ran with their tents and belongings to higher ground.

"The storm soon arrived, just as Eagle had predicted. The waves crashed against the shore and soon the site of the village, were we are standing now, was washed out to sea.

"With the village gone, the waves started crashing against the wooden walls surrounding Selfish Man's tent. Quickly the ground beneath the walls washed away. With nothing to hold them up, the walls collapsed, and

Selfish Man's tent and coins were all washed out to sea. His coins sank to the bottom, where they turned into Sand Dollars."

Grandfather looked down at Grandson and said, "Because he would not give a little to help others, Selfish Man lost everything.

"Now, after every storm we still find Sand Dollars here, as a reminder that money is most valuable when it is used to help others as well as yourself."

Deer's Antlers

Granddaughter climbed among the boulders on the beach. Each place she looked brought a new discovery. The tide pools revealed tiny fish and crabs, and the birds overhead created a symphony of sound.

For a long time, Grandmother watched and thought about the many things that she had learned since she was Granddaughter's age.

Granddaughter came up from the beach with a handful of clams and sat down beside her.

She said to Grandmother, "I have been watching the birds. I noticed that Seagull could find clams by tapping on the sand with his beak to make them squirt up water. So I tried tapping the sand with a stick and look at all the clams I found!"

Grandmother said to her, "That is a valuable lesson you have learned."

At the edge of the forest, a little distance away, Deer emerged and looked over at them.

"You are discovering more about our world every day, just like Deer.

"When Deer first came to this world he did not have big antlers. Deer did not know very much about the world, but like you, he wanted to learn.

"Some things he learned from his mother. For example, she taught him that he could find food during the winter snows by looking under the big tree branches in the forest where the snow was not so deep. That is when Deer's first antler spike emerged.

"Other things he learned from his father, like where to find the path to climb up to the high alpine meadows in early summer. That is when Deer's second antler spike grew.

"Many things Deer learned from experience. Whenever something would happen, Deer would ask himself, 'What can I learn from this?'

"When he broke through the early fall ice that formed on the edge of the stream, he said to himself, 'I must remember to wait for the ice to get thick enough before I try to walk on it.' Another spike was added to his antlers.

"When he was chased by Cougar, he said to himself, 'I must always be on the lookout for where Cougar is hunting and stay out of his way.' And another spike grew in.

"When he found some sweet moss hanging from the branches of a tree, he said, 'I will remember this spot when my family cannot find any grass to eat.' Yet another spike emerged.

"Today we can see how many lessons he has learned by looking at his big crown of antlers.

"So, Granddaughter, it is good that you are learning from your experiences and, just like Deer, finding a lesson in each one."

Moose's Pace

Father was hurrying to get ready to leave the camp down by the ocean. He was packing up bags, closing up windows, and carrying things out of the house. The more he rushed about, the more upset he became.

He shouted to Grandmother, "Hurry. We must be ready to go first thing tomorrow morning as soon as the sun rises."

Grandmother called him over and said, "Come and sit with me and have a cup of tea. I need to tell you a story."

Father replied, "I do not have time to sit down or to hear a story. I have to finish getting ready."

Grandmother said to him, "This will not take too long."

Father sat down, and as Grandmother passed him his cup of tea, she started her story.

"Many years ago there was a young man who ran wherever he went. He never walked – always ran at full speed.

"Now, for some things, that was good. If someone had an urgent message to get to someone else they would always give it to the young man, because they knew that he would run all the way to deliver it. When important things needed to be done in a hurry, he was always the one they would ask.

"People started to give him more and more things to run about doing – including some things that were not really very important. At first he could handle the extra work, but after a while he started to get more and more tired. Now, when they gave him something important to deliver quickly, he did not have enough energy to run full speed all the way. People started to complain. The young man tried to keep running, even when he knew he needed to rest.

"One day when the young man was running to the next village with a very heavy package, the last of his energy ran out and he fell to the ground.

"Eagle, who had been watching the man for a long time, flew down to his side and with a touch of his wing feathers transformed him into Moose.

"Eagle said to Moose, 'I have changed you into a big, slow animal who is not very good at running. You will have to take your time to wander slowly through the forest and to swim with your mate in the warm water of the lake. At a slower pace you will have time to enjoy all the beauty and friends around you that you missed when you used to rush around. Remember to save your energy for things that are truly important.'"

Father thought about Moose then smiled at Grandmother and said, "I think I know what your story is trying to tell me. I have been running too much. When I think about it, I can see it really does not matter if we leave as soon as the sun rises. I have forgotten to take time to appreciate the most important things in life – people, like you, and the beauty of nature around me."

Cedar Tree's Roots

The cold winter wind howled around the cabin and crept in through the cracks between the logs. Grandmother and Grandfather sat in front of the fireplace. They were warm under a goose-down comforter.

Off in the forest a tree cracked. Then came the sound of it crashing to the ground.

Grandfather said, "Sounds like Alder Tree has fallen. I always thought he grew too fast. When times were good, he never made the effort to grow his roots. Now it is too late. In the first bad storm he has fallen."

Grandmother said, "The wind is testing the strength of all the trees tonight. I hope that Cedar Tree does not blow down."

Grandfather replied, "Cedar Tree can withstand the biggest winds of winter. For many years she has grown roots deep down into the soil, knowing that some day she would need that strength to help her through bad times. She may not be as tall and wide as Alder Tree was, but she is standing proud while he is down."

Grandmother smiled and said, "Not unlike us, Grandfather. Years ago when we first met, we started putting down our own roots. We built this home, raised our children, and always treated each other with respect and love."

Grandfather nodded in agreement and said, "Yes, and that strong foundation has weathered us through some stormy times. We have always come out standing proud."

About the Author

Born in Vancouver, BC, in 1953, Robert James (Jim) Challenger has lived all of his life near the rugged Pacific coast. He is the son of proud fourth-generation Canadians who raised their children to appreciate nature and the lessons that can be learned from it.

Jim spent his childhood summers on Thetis Island, where he began to study and appreciate the unique wildlife, fish, and birds that inhabit the Pacific Northwest and BC west coast. Moving to Victoria, BC, in 1973, Jim met his wife, Joannie, a schoolteacher, and they built their home among the evergreens near the Strait of Juan de Fuca. They have two daughters, Kristi and Kari.

In this peaceful coastal setting, with the majesty of the Olympic Peninsula on the horizon, Jim's artistic side flourished. A strong admirer of historic First Nations and Native American art and legends, he began designing his own images. Jim developed a special process to carve his designs into the rounded stones found on the windswept beaches of the Pacific. Patrons worldwide have enjoyed not only Jim's beautiful carvings but also the stories that inspired them. His stone carvings are owned by collectors across Canada, Japan, Europe, South America, and the United States.

With the images to inspire him, he created a collection of fables that his daughters and their grandparents might enjoy.

Jim's stories bring a unique perspective to lessons we can learn from nature and the world around us. They are stories that are meant to be shared and enjoyed among family and friends. For more information about the author, visit www.rjchallenger.com.